For Gabriel – C F

For Mum 'n' Pop – S M

LITTLE TIGER PRESS
An imprint of Magi Publications
1 The Coda Centre, 189 Munster Road, London SW6 6AW
www.littletigerpress.com

First published in Great Britain 2008
This edition published in 2008

Text copyright © Claire Freedman 2008
Illustrations copyright © Simon Mendez 2008
Claire Freedman and Simon Mendez have asserted their rights
to be identified as the author and illustrator of this work
under the Copyright, Designs and Patents Act, 1988

A CIP catalogue record for this book is available from the British Library

Printed in China

2 4 6 8 10 9 7 5 3

On This Special Night

Claire Freedman   Simon Mendez

LITTLE TIGER PRESS
London

It was a silent winter's night. Frosty trees glistened
in the shadowy twilight. High above, the heavens
sparkled, watching, watching . . .

   Little Kitten was snuggled up in the old, wooden
barn. Outside, stars studded the inky-blue sky.
The wind hushed, barely a whisper, waiting, waiting . . .

"Cuddle up closer," Mother Cat said. "Try and go to sleep."

"But the stars are so bright tonight," cried Little Kitten.

One star was bigger than the rest. Blazing with a brilliant light, it seemed to fill the heavens.

"That must be a special star," Mother Cat whispered.

Just at that moment, a gentle crackle of leaves broke through the stillness of the night.

"Could I trouble you for some water?" asked Donkey, nudging open the door. "I've been travelling all day and I'm thirsty."

"Of course," said Mother Cat kindly. "And you are welcome to stay in the barn with us tonight."

"Thank you," Donkey smiled. "But I am on a very special journey." And he trundled out into the soft, silver moonlight.

Little Kitten watched, wondering . . .

Just then Little Kitten heard a gentle *Baa! Baa!*

"I've walked such a long way," bleated Lamb, "and I'm oh-so tired. Could I rest for a while in your comfy hay?"

"Why, of course," Mother Cat smiled.

So Lamb curled up with his new friends, cosy, calm, and peaceful.

Outside, high in the sky, the biggest, brightest
star blazed on, watching, waiting . . .
"Do you know why that star is so bright
tonight?" Little Kitten asked Lamb.

"Oh yes!" whispered Lamb.
"I can tell you a story
about that star . . ."

But before Lamb could begin, there came a *Scritch!*
Scratch! Scritch! Scratch! and three tiny mice
peered through a crack in the wall.

"May we snuggle up with you?" they shivered.
"We've been walking forever, and our paws
are frozen!"

"It's time I carried on my journey," Lamb said softly.
And silently he tiptoed away.

The mice nestled down, out of the bitter cold,
sharing the shelter of the snug, cosy bed.

"Where are you travelling to?" Little Kitten
asked. "Are you following the star?"

But before they could answer, there came
a *Moo! Moooo!* and Calf peeped his head round
the battered door. Another visitor!

"Do you have any food to spare?" Calf asked. "I've not had time to eat this evening."

There was plenty of fresh hay and Calf
chewed hungrily. "Thank you," he mumbled.
"I can't stay long; I must be on my way."
The mice stretched and yawned.
"We must hurry too," they said.
"But where are you all
going?" Little Kitten cried.

Calf smiled, his big, brown eyes shining.
"Tonight is a very special night," he said.
"Something amazing is going to happen."
"Come with us – and you'll see it too!"
squeaked the mice.

"Oh can we, Mummy?" begged Little Kitten.
But it was very late, so Mother Cat and
Little Kitten climbed to the top of the
barn roof to see what they could see.

High on the roof, the air was crisp and
clear and cold. Little Kitten gazed in wonder at
the sparkling, starlit sky. It felt as if the whole world
were holding its breath, watching, waiting . . .

"Look, Mummy!" Little Kitten cried.

There, silhouetted against the dark night sky, walked
three magnificent camels.

"This is a *very* special night!" Mother Cat whispered.
"Come on, Little Kitten. Let's go and see what's happening."

Shadows softened in the still night air as
Mother Cat and Little Kitten reached the
bottom of the hill. There stood a simple
stable, aglow in the light of the shining star.
 "Let's go in!" whispered the animals in
hushed excitement.

Tenderly, Mother Cat helped Little Kitten
squeeze inside. His heart burst with happiness
at what he saw: a baby! It was sleeping soundly
in the sweet, soft hay.

This was a very special baby.
   The animals watched quietly as above them
all, the bright, bright star blazed in the night . . .
shining with peace
                    and joy
                         and love.

Read these other special titles by Little Tiger Press

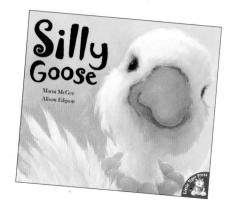

For information regarding any of the above
titles or for our catalogue, please contact us:
Little Tiger Press, 1 The Coda Centre,
189 Munster Road, London SW6 6AW
Tel: 020 7385 6333 Fax: 020 7385 7333
E-mail: info@littletiger.co.uk
www.littletigerpress.com